About the Author

Dale lives in the beautiful Fraser Valley in beautiful British Columbia. Did he mention it is beautiful there? He likes to spend long periods of time in the local woods and forest, which is a good thing because he is usually lost, unless he is with his wife who is part homing pigeon. He has two grown sons whom he has taught the life saving skills of always being prepared for the unknown by taking them down paths unknown... and getting lost. When not lost in the woods you can find him wandering the banks of the river probably heading in the wrong direction.

Dale Niles

Elad's Fables: Dahlia The Dragon

Nightingale Books

A CIP catalogue record for this title is
available from the British Library.

ISBN 9781838751135

Nightingale Books is an imprint of
Pegasus Elliot MacKenzie Publishers Ltd.
www.pegasuspublishers.com

First Published in 2021

Nightingale Books
Sheraton House Castle Park
Cambridge England

Printed & Bound in Great Britain

Dedication

Dedicated to my long suffering, short memory, quick laughing, slow burning, high minded, low reaching, one and only love and wife of my life, Monica.
This book is her fault.

Dahlia the Dragon was
green, young, and strong,
He was happy with life,
there was just one thing wrong.

All the other young dragons
laughed and made song,
Of how Dahlia the Dragon
was somehow named wrong!

Dahlia's all right if
you're naming a flower,
A girl or a pixie
with magical power.

But the name of a dragon
should make all things cower!
Like Slayer or Darthron
or Demon or Gower!

Dahlia decided he
needed a quest,
He would look for a knight
who wanted a test.

Dahlia would fight him
and prove who was best,
Then all of the dragons
would want him as guest!

Dahlia set off,
he needed a knight,
One strong and brave
and willing to fight!

Because this was the way
to fix Dahlia's plight,
Dahlia soared to the castle
and hoped he was right!

Dahlia flew to the castle
and let out a roar.
"Send me a knight
who wants to be lore,

One who is brave
with no fear of gore!"
Dahlia spat out some flames
then sat down at the door.

Dahlia sat through the
day and into the next,
He sat there so long he
at last became vexed.

It looked with his name
he was totally hexed.
So here he was stuck
between and betwext.

As Dahlia sat at the gate,
with the sun on his head,
He became very sleepy
and wishing for bed.

Before he knew it his head
was like lead,
He fell fast asleep and
looked as though dead.

T'was then that a knight
did dare to draw near,
His armour did rattle
so great was his fear.

Closer he came with
his sword and his spear,
If he killed the dragon the
whole castle would cheer!

But as he came near
young Dahlia did wake,
He peeked through long lashes
to see who would bake.

The knight saw him peeking
and started to shake,
The knight's only thought was,
'How long would it take?'

The dragon roared,
"What is your name,
I will write it in blood
and increase both our fame.

I'll roast you alive and
all others the same,
Speak up brave knight and
I'll end this game."

The knight stood tall and
called, "My name is Rose,
And if you think you can bake
me we'll see how it goes.

A career slaying dragon
is one that I chose,
So let's see who's best when it
comes down to blows!"

"WHAT!" roared the dragon.
"Say it's not true?
A knight who's named Rose?
I can NOT bake you.

The news I killed a Rose
well that just won't do,
Send some other knight,
there must be a few?"

Rose said, "A knight with my
name is just no big deal,
It's not in the name and
it's not how you feel.

It's the fire inside,
it's the spirit that's real,
You'd better get lost or
your hide I will peel!"

Dahlia roared out in anger
and let out a blast,
But you must hand it to Rose,
he moved pretty fast!

He stepped to one side
and the flame sailed past,
So they fought through the
day till the sun set at last.

Dahlia was tired and Rose
leaned on his sword,
But Rose was not burned,
and Dahlia not gored.

Throughout the fight they
were watched by a hoard,
And all would agree that
they hadn't been bored.

Dahlia now realized that
Rose had been right.
Your name's not important
if you use all your might.

Dahlia decided his name's
not his plight,
It's not strength, or size,
but it's spirit and fight.

Dahlia stepped back
and took a great bow,
Poor Rose just thought,
'What happens now?'

He picked up a flag and
wiped off his brow
And a line in the sand with
his sword he did plough.

But Dahlia the Dragon
had made other plans,
He took to the sky with
the sound of great fans.

Rose turned to the crowd
and raised both his hands,
Then the crowd did rejoice
and struck up the bands.

Now Dahlia's at home
content with his fate,
He knows in his heart that
he's not second rate.

And though he's not rich
he has a lot on his plate,
When he looks in the mirror
he sees 'Dahlia the Great'!

Manufactured by Amazon.ca
Bolton, ON